THE PUPPY PLACE

DONUT

THE PUPPY PLACE

Don't miss any of these other stories by Ellen Miles!

Angel
Bandit
Barney
Baxter
Bear
Bella
Bentley
Biggie
Bitsy
Bonita
Boomer
Bubbles and Boo
Buddy
Champ
Chewy and Chica
Cocoa
Cody
Cooper
Cuddles
Daisy
Edward
Flash
Fluffy & Freckles
Gizmo
Goldie
Gus
Honey
Jack
Jake
Kodiak
Liberty
Lily
Lola
Louie
Lucky
Lucy
Maggie and Max
Miki
Mocha
Molly
Moose
Muttley
Nala
Noodle
Oscar
Patches
Princess
Pugsley
Rascal
Rocky
Roxy
Rusty
Scout
Shadow
Snowball
Sparky
Spirit
Stella
Sugar, Gummi, and Lollipop
Sweetie
Teddy
Ziggy
Zipper

THE PUPPY PLACE

DONUT

SCHOLASTIC INC.

Cover art by Tim O'Brien
Original cover design by Steve Scott

ISBN 978-1-338-68702-6

10 9 8 7 6 5 4 3 2 1 21 22 23 24 25

Printed in the U.S.A. 40
First printing 2021

CHAPTER ONE

"Here's Buckley!" Lizzie Peterson led an excited Yorkie into the reception area at Bowser's Backyard, her aunt's doggy day-care center. Buckley pulled at the leash when he saw who was waiting for him.

"Buckley!" The woman knelt down and opened her arms, and Lizzie let the leash drop so the little dog could dash into his owner's embrace. Lizzie loved seeing people and their dogs reunited at the end of the day. It was her favorite time to help out at Aunt Amanda's—especially on Fridays, when the people and dogs were looking forward to being together all weekend.

"Buckley was a good boy today," Lizzie told his owner. "I hear he had a lot of fun with Lena and Skye." Lena and Skye were sister puppies, almost but not quite identical. They were both happy, fluffy, bouncy poodle mixes with pretty brown-and-cream coats. Lizzie knew that they both loved to play.

"Buckley loves it here," said his owner, smiling at Lizzie. "But I'm glad I get him to myself for two whole days now."

"Bye, Buckley, have a great weekend!" said Lizzie. She waved good-bye to Buckley as she went back to the kennels to fetch another dog whose owner was waiting.

Lizzie was excited about the upcoming weekend, too. Her aunt had invited her to Camp Bowser, her doggy sleepaway camp in the country. They would be driving up tomorrow, and Lizzie couldn't wait. It was always a treat to spend time there with Aunt Amanda, who was possibly the only person in the world more dog-crazy than Lizzie. Aunt Amanda knew so much about dogs, and was always happy to share her knowledge with Lizzie.

Lizzie had loved dogs for as long as she could remember. She loved playing with them, training them, cuddling with them, and learning about them. Besides helping her aunt, she also volunteered at the local animal shelter, and she even had a dog-walking business. On top of all that, she and her younger brothers, Charles and the Bean, had managed to convince their parents to let them foster puppies. Now the Petersons were a foster family who took care of puppies who needed homes.

Best of all, Lizzie had her own puppy, the best puppy ever. Buddy had started out as a foster puppy, but when the whole family had fallen in love, they had decided to keep him forever.

"Can Buddy come to Camp Bowser with us?" she asked her aunt as they got ready to sweep and mop the kennels after all the dogs had left.

"Aw, I love Buddy, you know that," said Aunt Amanda. "But this time it's just going to be us and Bowser, remember? We have a lot to do if we're going to plan that clicker-training workshop."

Lizzie nodded. "Right," she said. "Got it." She was flattered that Aunt Amanda had asked for her help this weekend. They were going to work on a new workshop that her aunt wanted to start offering. Lizzie had heard of clicker training, but she'd never tried it—which, according to Aunt Amanda, was perfect. Lizzie hoped she wouldn't let Aunt Amanda down.

"You and Bowser will be learning at the same time," her aunt had said. "We'll keep a training diary and see how much we can do in one weekend. And if I'm right about my guess, we can make it so simple that even kids can take the workshop. Of course, most kids don't know nearly as much as you do about dogs, but still."

Lizzie felt herself blushing. Compliments from her aunt meant so much. It was one thing for your parents to tell you how fantastic you were—that was kind of their job, really. But to have Aunt Amanda compliment her—well, that was extra special.

Aunt Amanda really was a dog expert. She had Bowser, a big, calm, older golden retriever, who was always up for anything. She also had three pugs, but this weekend they would be staying home with Uncle James. "We don't need all that wild pug energy when we're trying to concentrate," she said now as she wrung out the mop.

"Remind me again about how it works?" Lizzie asked. "The clicker thing?"

"It's simple, really," said her aunt. She pulled a small rectangular device out of her pocket and pressed on it with her thumb. A sharp *click* rang out. “Once a dog learns that this sound,” she clicked again, “means the same as ‘good dog’ and that a treat is coming, you can train them quickly to do all sorts of things.”

“But why is it better than just saying ‘good dog’?” Lizzie asked.

“Well, because it’s loud, and it’s a particular sound that doesn’t sound like anything else,” said her aunt. “It’s very clear, and you can time it exactly so the dog knows just what it is that he’s doing right.” She smiled at Lizzie as they hung up the mop and broom. “You’ll see. I think you’ll love it. Take a look online tonight if you want. I’ll send you links to some of my favorite clicker trainers’ videos.”

Just then, Aunt Amanda’s phone rang. “Hello?” she said, putting the phone to her ear.

Lizzie watched as her aunt listened, her expression becoming more and more concerned.

"Hi, Mac. Oh, dear. Poor Donut. I can just imagine. How can I help?" She looked upset. "This weekend? Now? Well . . . sure. Yes. Of course." She hung up and turned to Lizzie.

"What happened?" Lizzie asked.

"Do you remember Donut?" asked Aunt Amanda. "That little German shepherd–Lab mix? The sweetest pup."

Lizzie nodded. "She was in your puppy kindergarten a while ago, right?" Lizzie loved helping out at puppy kindergarten classes. It was always so much fun to see the youngest dogs try hard to please their owners—when all they really wanted to do was bark, run around like wild things, and wrestle with one another. It was total chaos, total joy.

"That's right," said Aunt Amanda. "And they've been regulars here since then. But now her family has to move across country for a job. They've found a great home to rent, but . . ."

"They don't allow dogs," said Lizzie. She'd heard it before at the animal shelter. It was one of the most common reasons why people had to give up their dogs. Lizzie felt bad for the family—but she also felt a familiar little tickle of excitement. "So maybe they need a foster family for Donut?" she asked.

"Not quite yet," said Aunt Amanda. "They're still hoping for a miracle. But time is running out. They're packing up all their belongings this weekend, and Mac says that Donut is getting very upset. She knows something's going on. He asked me to take her for the weekend. So—"

"So we get to take her to camp with us?" Lizzie asked. She felt sorry for Donut's owners, but she couldn't help being excited, too. "Maybe we can try clicker training her, too."

Her aunt looked at her and nodded. "You know," she said, "that's actually not a bad idea at all."

The front door buzzer sounded just then, and Aunt Amanda went to unlock the door. A man came in, holding one end of a leash. At the other end was an adorable, roly-poly, brown-and-black puppy.

"Donut!" Lizzie said, kneeling down.

CHAPTER TWO

Donut trotted right into Lizzie's arms, her tail wagging so hard that her whole body wagged along with it.

I know a friend when I see one!

Lizzie let the puppy sniff her hands, then petted her gently. Her brown-and-black fur—touched with golden highlights—was so thick and soft. Donut had shining golden-brown eyes, the color of honey. Her ears tried to stand up but mostly flopped over. She was a sturdy, solidly built little pup who seemed to want nothing more than to please.

The puppy wriggled happily while Lizzie petted her all over. "Good girl," Lizzie whispered. "That's a good girl."

"That's right, she is a good girl," said the man holding the leash. "Donut is . . . well, she's just the best."

Lizzie looked up at him and realized that he was crying. Really crying. She felt her heart flip over in her chest. This man really loved his dog.

Lizzie had seen her dad cry during the sad part of a movie or when he was watching Charles in a school play or listening to the Bean sing a new song he'd learned. Sometimes Dad even cried during this one really sappy commercial on TV.

When Lizzie's dad cried, it was just a few tears sliding quietly down his face. If you weren't watching closely, you wouldn't even know. But this man, here in the reception area at Bowser's Backyard, was sobbing.

"Oh, Mac," said Aunt Amanda, putting an arm around his shoulder. "It's so hard. I just hate to see this happen."

"Wanda and the kids are taking it even harder," Mac said between sobs. "We just don't know how we're going to manage without Donut. We all love her so much." He took a deep breath and put his shoulders back. "But this job Wanda's been offered—it's just too good to pass up. It's what she deserves, and we're all excited to be moving to California. We really are. Except . . ." He knelt down next to Lizzie and pulled Donut into his arms. Then he cried some more, burying his face in her neck. His whole body shook.

Donut snuffled Mac's face all over and licked the tears off his cheeks.

Don't be sad! I'll make you feel better.

Lizzie looked up at Aunt Amanda, and saw that her aunt had tears in her eyes. So did Lizzie. This was just heartbreaking to see.

"Maybe you could find another place, one that takes dogs?" Lizzie asked.

Mac looked up. "We've tried," he said tiredly. "There just isn't much to choose from. Our kids need space to play and a good school to go to, and we're going to try to get by with just one car." He hugged Donut one more time and stood up. "It's such a shame," he said, wiping his eyes on his sleeve, "because the place we found is absolutely perfect for a dog. It has a fenced yard, it's near a park with a beautiful river running through it, and there are all sorts of hiking trails to explore. Donut would have been so happy there." He shook his head, looking down at his puppy. She looked back up at him and thumped her tail, cocking her head to one side. She put up a paw, as if begging him to tell her what was wrong.

Is there a problem? Can I help?

"But?" Aunt Amanda prompted. "What happened?"

"I don't know," said Mac. "I was in touch with the landlord, the man who owns the property. They live in the house next door, and he seemed fine with us bringing Donut. Then all of a sudden, he told me that we couldn't have a dog after all, that his wife wasn't comfortable with it."

Lizzie gasped, but Aunt Amanda nodded. "Some people just don't get dogs," she said. "Sometimes they're afraid because of something that happened when they were younger, and sometimes they've just never been around a well-behaved, lovable dog like Donut. They think all dogs are mean or messy or destructive."

"That's why I gave him your name as a reference," Mac said. "I knew you would vouch for Donut."

Aunt Amanda shook her head. "I know, I remember the e-mail you copied me on. And of course I would have told him what a great dog Donut is, but he never wrote to ask me," Aunt Amanda said. "I guess the decision was already made."

Donut had been watching the people talk, her gaze moving from one face to the other. Her eyes were serious. She pushed her nose into Mac's hand and leaned against him.

I can't stand it when my people are upset. Maybe they just need more cuddles.

Lizzie took a breath. "I know you may not be ready to hear this," she said to Mac, "but when—I mean, if—you decide it's time to find Donut the perfect new home, my family can help. We foster puppies, and we take really good care of them until we are sure we've found each one the right forever family."

Mac began to cry again. "You're right," he said between sniffles. "I'm not ready to hear that. But I'm glad to know that you can help if we need it." He bent to hug Donut one more time. "This isn't good-bye," he told her. "We'll see you on Sunday night." He straightened up. "I just think it'll be much easier on all of us if she doesn't have to watch us pack up the whole house. Dogs know when something's going on. I don't want her to worry."

"We'll take great care of her until Sunday night," Aunt Amanda told him. "Remember that clicker-training workshop I told you about? Lizzie is going to help me with it this weekend. We'll keep Donut busy learning new things, so she won't miss you too much."

Mac nodded, gave Donut one more pat, and stood to go. "Wanda's probably wondering what's taking me so long," he said. "I'd better get back and help with the packing."

"And I'd better call my mom to make sure it's okay to bring a puppy home tonight," Lizzie said.

Mac stopped in his tracks and raised an eyebrow. "You want to take her home with you?" he asked.

Lizzie nodded. Of course she did.

Aunt Amanda had also looked surprised, but after a moment, she spoke up. "You know, the Petersons are actually kind of puppy experts," she told Mac. "It'll be quieter over there than in the kennels here, and since Donut is feeling upset, it would be nice for her to be with a family. I can't take her home with me because the pugs would drive her nuts." She shrugged. "Might be the best idea," she said to Mac, "if it's okay with you."

Mac peered at Lizzie. Then he nodded. "Sure. Call your mom and make sure it's okay."

Lizzie turned and dashed for the phone, grinning. She knew Mom would say yes. It was only for one night—at least for now.

A few minutes later, when Mac had left, Aunt Amanda put an arm around Lizzie. "That was tough," she said. "I really feel for them."

"Me, too," said Lizzie. She petted Donut, who sat staring at the door with sad eyes, as if she expected Mac to change his mind and walk back in. "It'll be okay, girl," Lizzie said softly to the puppy. "It'll be okay."

CHAPTER THREE

Donut fit in perfectly at Lizzie's house. She and Buddy were instant pals, racing around the backyard two seconds after they'd met. "Isn't she great?" Lizzie asked Charles and the Bean, who had come out to meet Donut.

"How could anybody give her up?" Charles asked. "She's so cute!"

The Bean laughed his gurgly laugh as he watched the puppies wrestle. "We keep that uppy! She can be Buddy's sister," he pronounced.

"Um," said Lizzie. Sometimes it was hard for the Bean to understand what fostering really meant:

that they had to give up every "uppy," even if it was hard. And it was always hard. Some puppies made it even harder—and Lizzie could already tell that Donut was one of them.

Charles laughed. "Maybe it's time to work on Mom and Dad again," he said. "Maybe we actually could keep Donut, if her owners decide she needs a new home. I think the Bean's right—Buddy deserves a sibling. After all, I have two, and so do both of you. Why shouldn't Buddy?"

Lizzie grinned. "True," she said. "But you know Mom and Dad will just say no. Or tell us that if we have two permanent dogs, we can't foster puppies anymore." She put her head to one side. "Still . . . did you see the way Mom looked at Donut?" She made a face with lovey-dovey goo-goo eyes, and both Charles and the Bean burst out laughing.

"You look exactly like Mom when you do that!" Charles said. "I mean, exactly like Mom when she really falls for a puppy."

Lizzie grinned. "I have a feeling Dad will like Donut, too. He's a big fan of Labrador retrievers and German shepherds. What could be better than a mix?"

Buddy and Donut raced over, panting. They climbed all over Lizzie and her brothers, kissing their noses and snuffling their cheeks. The Bean giggled and shrieked.

"They're so happy together," Lizzie said, after she'd thrown a ball and watched the puppies dash off after it. "I think all this playing is taking Donut's mind off what's happening with her family. But it's sad. Donut's true perfect home is with Mac and Wanda and their kids. I know they really love her and don't want to give her up. It's not fair!" She had told Charles about the way Mac had cried when he said good-bye to Donut.

After dinner, Lizzie took Donut upstairs with her. She'd begged her mom for some screen time so she could research clicker training and maybe check out a few of the training videos Aunt Amanda had told her about. Now that she had Donut to train, Lizzie was more excited than ever about the upcoming weekend. The puppy went straight to the dog bed Mom kept under her desk, curled up on it, and went to sleep. Lizzie's heart swelled when she looked down at the pup. She did look just like a little donut when she was all curled up like that.

"You're all tuckered out, aren't you?" Lizzie asked, reaching down to pet Donut while she waited for a video to load. "You and Buddy know how to tire each other out!"

Donut's feet twitched and she made a funny

little whining noise, so Lizzie knew she was already dreaming. Lizzie always wondered what dogs dream about.

"Probably chasing squirrels," Dad had said when she'd wondered out loud one day. "Or sometimes chipmunks. Or if they have a nightmare, maybe they're the ones being chased."

Lizzie hoped Donut was not having a nightmare. She smiled down at the pup, then turned to watch the video. "Wow," she said as she watched a trainer teach a dog to play dead in about four minutes, using a clicker. "Amazing!" She watched another video, and another, then read some tips on how to get started. The first step for clicker training was to teach the dog that the clicking noise meant "yay for you!" All you needed was a handful of really good treats. It sounded so easy. Lizzie looked down at Donut, still sleeping. Lizzie bit her lip. She really wanted to try it—just that first step. Should she or shouldn't she? It was getting late. Any minute now her parents were going to tell her it was time for bed. Plus, she had to pack for the weekend. But . . .

She watched the "first step" video one more time and made up her mind.

Five minutes later, Lizzie was stepping very quietly down the stairs. She slipped into the kitchen and opened the fridge. She needed something really yummy for training treats. "Aha!" The leftover chicken from that night's dinner. "Perfect," she said to herself. She grabbed a piece of white meat off the plate and quickly wrapped the rest of the chicken up and put it back. Then she tiptoed back upstairs. She knew Mom probably wouldn't mind if she took the chicken, but still.

"Pssst, hey, Donut!" Lizzie said, reaching under Mom's desk to give the sleeping pup a nudge.

"Want to try something fun?" She had already stopped in to her room to find the clicker Aunt Amanda had loaned her. She'd wrapped it up in a sock, and now she put it behind her back, two tricks she'd learned from the videos. "Some dogs find the loud noise of the clicker upsetting," one of the trainers had said. "Muffle the sound with some cloth, and don't click it right in your pup's face."

Donut looked up at Lizzie, blinking sleepily.

Is this important? Because I was just about to catch that squirrel . . .

Behind her back, Lizzie clicked the clicker, then immediately gave Donut her treat: a tiny piece of chicken, about the size of a pea, the way the trainer had advised. Donut gobbled it down and looked up at Lizzie.

That was yummy! Is there more?

"Good girl." Lizzie stood up. Donut got up, too, the cozy bed forgotten. She snuffled at Lizzie's hand, hoping for more treats.

"See? Fun! Come on." Lizzie stepped back and patted her own leg. She clicked again and tossed Donut another shred of chicken. Click, treat. Click, treat. Again. Again. Again. Donut gobbled up each piece then immediately looked back up at Lizzie, her intelligent eyes gleaming.

When Lizzie had done it ten times, she dropped the clicker and knelt to hug Donut. "Good girl!" she said. "What a good girl. I think you've already got it!" She could tell that Donut already knew that the clicking sound meant something good.

Then Lizzie had a sudden thought. Had *she* done something good? Or was it wrong to have started

Donut's training? Aunt Amanda had wanted to start from scratch. Lizzie reached down to ruffle Donut's ears. "Oh, well," she said. "I guess it's too late now."

CHAPTER FOUR

"All set?" Aunt Amanda asked.

Lizzie gave her a thumbs-up, and Aunt Amanda backed her big silver SUV out of the driveway. Lizzie's family waved good-bye. Lizzie smiled and waved back, even though she knew they were mostly waving at Donut. It was Saturday morning, and they were on their way to Camp Bowser.

Bowser and Donut were snug on cushy sheepskin beds inside two of the dog crates in the way-back. They both seemed to understand that it was time to settle in for a while, and after a happy greeting, they had each curled up for a snooze.

"How did Donut sleep last night?" asked Aunt Amanda. She seemed to assume that Donut had slept in Lizzie's room—which, of course, was true.

"I think she had some nightmares," Lizzie said. "She was whining a lot in her sleep. But mostly she was calm."

"Poor little girl," said Aunt Amanda, looking up at the rearview mirror to check on the dogs. "I know she's very attached to her family. Labs are like that, and so are German shepherds. They really bond with their people."

"I've heard that before," said Lizzie. "And I know her people are really bonded with her, too." They were both quiet for a moment, thinking about the sad scene from the night before.

"Music?" Aunt Amanda asked, once they were on the highway. She pointed to the radio.

Lizzie shook her head. She wasn't in the mood. She looked at her aunt, wondering if she should tell her now or later that she had already started to train Donut. *Later*, she decided. She wanted to put it off, in case Aunt Amanda was mad.

"Tell me about the first dog you ever had," she said instead, knowing that this was the perfect way to get Aunt Amanda talking. Once you got her going on dogs, Aunt Amanda could talk forever.

"Oh, Peanut," said Aunt Amanda, laughing. "You would have loved him. He was the cutest, goofiest basset hound ever. His ears were so long they dragged on the ground, but he didn't care. He followed your dad and me everywhere."

It was easy to keep Aunt Amanda talking, all the way until she turned onto a dirt lane that wound through a dark, piney-smelling forest. In the back, Bowser sat up and sniffed. "He knows where we are," said Aunt Amanda as she pulled up to a cozy cabin set in a clearing in the woods.

"I'm going to let him run, but let's keep Donut on a leash at first."

Lizzie remembered Aunt Amanda's routine at Camp Bowser. Before she unpacked anything or even went into the cabin, she always took the dogs down to the stream. "They've had a long car ride," she always said, "they deserve a run."

Lizzie got out and opened the back door. She opened Donut's crate and clipped a leash onto her collar. "C'mon, cutie," she said. "You're going to love it here." All dogs loved Camp Bowser. There was the stream, and plenty of woods to explore, and the screened-in Pooch Porch that was just perfect for napping on a hot summer day.

When Aunt Amanda opened his crate's door, Bowser leapt out, shook himself, and took off down the path, his feathery tail waving with delight. Aunt Amanda, Lizzie, and Donut followed behind. It was a warm day, with a breeze that stirred the leaves in the trees. Lizzie watched Donut take a deep sniff of the sweet-smelling air. She sniffed, too. "Ahhh," she said. "Camp Bowser. It's been a long time since I've been here."

"You haven't even seen the pond yet," said Aunt Amanda as they came around a bend in the trail. "Check it out!"

Lizzie had forgotten that Uncle James had dammed part of the stream in order to make a small pond for swimming or paddling in a canoe. "Wow!" she said when she saw it. "It's bigger than I pictured." She laughed as she watched Bowser run straight for the water's edge and plunge in. "He's a real water dog, isn't he?" she asked. "What about you, Donut? Are you a swimmer?"

Donut was more cautious. She approached the pond slowly, then pawed at the water. She looked around, as if hoping for someone to tell her what to do.

Um, not so sure about this. Maybe if my people were here, I would be a little braver . . .

"Good girl," said Lizzie. "Better to take it easy at first."

After both dogs had a good walk, Lizzie helped Aunt Amanda unpack the car. She felt the clicker in her pocket, and wondered when they would begin training. Sooner or later, Aunt Amanda was going to find out what she had done. She sighed with relief when Aunt Amanda said that they would have lunch first, then get the training area ready and set up for filming their sessions.

Aunt Amanda handed Lizzie a notebook. "I'll take care of the video, but I want you to keep the training diary," she said. "It'll really help when I start teaching the course."

"What do I write in it?" Lizzie asked, taking the notebook.

"Everything we do," said Aunt Amanda. "Starting from the very beginning."

Lizzie gulped. Was now the time to tell her aunt what she'd done?

But Aunt Amanda turned around and started pulling things out of a cooler. "Cheese, lettuce, tomatoes—how about if you get the dogs some food and water while I make us sandwiches?"

Lizzie just nodded and headed for the cabinet where the dog bowls were kept. The moment had passed.

After lunch, Aunt Amanda had Lizzie clear the dog beds off the Pooch Porch while she set up a tripod and got her phone ready to take videos.

"I cut up a bunch of cheese and some leftover steak that I brought," she told Lizzie. "We'll use that for treats."

Finally, it was time to start. "Ready?" Aunt Amanda asked. At lunchtime, she'd explained the first steps to Lizzie, and Lizzie had nodded and listened without admitting the truth. Now Aunt Amanda started filming, then nodded at Lizzie. "Call Donut over, and let's teach her what the clicker means."

Lizzie called Donut. She held the clicker behind her back and pressed her thumb into it. *Click.* Donut's head snapped up and she stared at Lizzie, head cocked, waiting for a treat. It was obvious that she already knew what that sound meant.

CHAPTER FIVE

Lizzie shot a look at Aunt Amanda. Maybe she hadn't noticed that Donut was already familiar with the clicker.

Aunt Amanda looked back at her, eyebrows raised. "Hmm," she said. "Interesting. Do it again."

Lizzie couldn't tell if her aunt was mad or not. She felt like running away, but instead she clicked the clicker. Donut snapped to attention, staring into Lizzie's eyes.

Yes? Where's my treat?

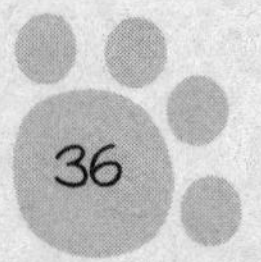

Lizzie tossed the puppy a treat. "Good girl," she said. Then she looked back at Aunt Amanda.

Her aunt was smiling. That was a good sign. Lizzie saw her reach over to turn off the camera. "So," said Aunt Amanda. "Looks like someone has already learned Step One."

Lizzie nodded, biting her lip. "I didn't really mean to do it," she said. "I just couldn't help myself. I was watching the videos and it seemed so simple—and it was. She's a really quick learner." She looked down at Donut, who was turning her head back and forth as she watched the conversation. She looked up at Lizzie and tilted her head to one side.

Aren't we going to keep going?

Aunt Amanda frowned for just a second, then shrugged. "Okay, well, you obviously did a good job," she said.

Lizzie sighed with relief. "You're not mad?" she asked.

Aunt Amanda laughed, shaking her head. "Well, of course I wish you'd told me before now–but I guess I'm too impressed to be really mad. Now, let's keep moving. You can do a few more rounds of clicking and treating with her, and then you can see how it works with Bowser." Bowser was taking an after-lunch nap in Aunt Amanda's spare bedroom—the one she called her yoga room—while he waited his turn.

She went back to turn the camera on. "Okay, click and treat," she said.

Lizzie clicked. She tossed treats. Donut was completely focused on Lizzie, ready to do whatever Lizzie asked. But for now, Lizzie wasn't asking for anything other than her attention. Click, treat. Click, treat. Click, treat. Donut did not take her eyes off Lizzie's.

"Fantastic," said Aunt Amanda. She turned off the camera again and came around to give Lizzie, and then Donut, big hugs. "You're both good girls," she said.

Lizzie felt herself glowing with pride.

"Now, let's see how it goes with Bowser," said Aunt Amanda. "This time, you'll really be starting from scratch."

"I'm ready," said Lizzie. She took Donut back to the yoga room and settled her in with a chew toy. "Let's go, Bowser," she said. "Your turn." Bowser seemed to be more interested in napping, but he finally got up, stretched, and followed Lizzie back out to the Pooch Porch.

This time, Aunt Amanda got the camera going, then came around in front and talked while Lizzie trained Bowser, explaining how this first step helped to teach the dog that the clicking sound meant a treat was coming soon. She nodded to Lizzie. “Okay, click and treat,” she said.

Lizzie clicked.

Bowser looked around for a moment, as if wondering where that new sound came from. Then he glanced up at Lizzie.

“Good boy!” Lizzie said, tossing him a treat. As soon as he’d gobbled it up, she clicked again. Click, treat. Click, treat. Bowser learned just as quickly as Donut had. Soon he was totally focused on Lizzie, just waiting for that next click and treat.

Aunt Amanda smiled. “Maybe you can teach an old dog new tricks, after all,” she said. “That’s great. We’ll click and treat just a few more times and then finish this session. It’s good to keep training sessions short, so our dogs don’t lose focus. And we always like to end on a good note.”

Lizzie clicked and treated a few more times. By now, Bowser was wide awake and really enjoying the new game. After her last click, Lizzie gave Bowser a whole bunch of treats at once—something Aunt Amanda had taught her. Dog trainers called it a "jackpot," just an extra big treat that came out of the blue. Lizzie knew that dogs loved it, and it was a great way to end this session. "Good boy," she said, throwing her arms around Bowser. He thumped his tail on the floor and grinned at her.

"The dogs deserve a break. Let's take them for a walk," said Aunt Amanda. "Then we'll come back and work on the next step."

Lizzie was ready for a break, too. Clicker training was fun, but you really had to focus on what you were doing. It was relaxing to step off the porch and head down the trail toward the pond. Lizzie smiled as she watched Bowser and Donut trotting down the path, shoulder to shoulder. "Donut is the kind of dog who wants to be friends with everyone she meets, isn't she?" Lizzie asked.

Her aunt nodded. "She's a real darling," she said.

Lizzie thought she heard something in her aunt's voice, a hint of yearning. "Would you and Uncle James ever adopt another dog?" she asked.

Aunt Amanda sighed. "I would, in a heartbeat. But silly old James thinks that four dogs is enough. Especially when three of them are pugs!" She laughed.

"Donut deserves a home as special as yours," Lizzie said.

Just then, Donut trotted back as if to check in on them. She snuffled at Lizzie's hand, then sat and looked up at her, tilting her head. Her eyes were questioning as she gazed at Lizzie.

You're not one of my people. I like you, but where are they, anyway? I can't be completely happy without them.

Lizzie had a feeling that Donut was missing her owners. She reached down to pet the puppy's soft, thick fur. "It's okay, girl," she said softly. "It's all going to be just fine." She didn't know how she could promise that, but she meant it with all her heart.

CHAPTER SIX

"Donut sure is one brave little girl," Lizzie said a half hour later as she and her aunt toweled off the two wet dogs in the cabin. "Only her second time at the pond and she jumped right in after Bowser."

"I wonder if she would go in the canoe," said Aunt Amanda. She told Lizzie that she'd been trying to convince Bowser to ride in her canoe with her. "I've seen people who take their dogs paddling on their kayaks and even on their stand-up paddleboards. I always thought it would be so much fun to have Bowser along in the canoe. Now I finally have a pond of my own and a canoe to paddle. But Bowser won't get in. He's terrified! It's too tippy, I think."

Lizzie couldn't blame Bowser. Canoes could be a little scary. "Would clicker training help?" she asked.

Aunt Amanda stared at her. "Lizzie Peterson, you are brilliant! Why didn't I think of that?"

Lizzie beamed.

"Maybe we can try after supper tonight," said Aunt Amanda. "If we have any energy left. I'll have to think about the best way to use the clicker . . ." She frowned, deep in thought already as she finished toweling Bowser off.

"Okay," she said, after they'd hung the towels out to dry. "Later for the canoe. It's time to get back to training."

"What do we do next, now that they know that the click means they've done a good job and there's a treat coming?" asked Lizzie as they set up for filming.

'Well, we start asking for a little more from the dogs. In order to get a click, they have to do something," said Aunt Amanda. "We won't even ask—we'll just wait to see what they offer. They've both had basic training, so they have some ideas about what humans might want them to do."

She handed Lizzie a handful of tiny soft bits. "Turkey I roasted yesterday," she said. "It's important to keep using really good treats as we move along. And they have to be small, like this"—she pointed to the pea-size pieces—"so the dog can eat them quickly and be ready for the next thing."

Lizzie nodded, taking it all in. "So I'm going to just stand there and wait until Bowser does something?" she asked. They'd decided that Bowser should go first this time. Donut was napping in the yoga room.

"Exactly," said Aunt Amanda. "And he will. You'll see. Trainers call it 'offering behaviors.' If dogs aren't sure what you want from them, they'll just run through all the stuff they know how to do."

Lizzie could never get over how much her aunt knew about dogs and dog training. And Aunt Amanda was right! When Lizzie and Bowser took their places in front of the camera, he looked up at her. When no click or treat came, he seemed to think for a second. Then he sat down and cocked his head at Lizzie.

"Click!" said Amanda, at the same time as Lizzie clicked. "Good, you get the idea," said her aunt. "Now praise him and give him a treat."

"Good boy," said Lizzie. She tossed Bowser a piece of meat.

After that, he lay down, stood up, offered a paw, and even rolled over, without Lizzie even asking.

She laughed as she clicked and treated for each new trick.

"Great," said Aunt Amanda, after a few minutes. "Let's quit for now and give Donut a turn. I warn you, she may be a little more challenging. She's a puppy, after all."

Aunt Amanda was right again, as it turned out. Donut was full of energy after her nap. She didn't want to focus. She wanted to bounce around and sniff everything. She wanted to chase her tail. She wanted to nibble on Lizzie's fingers.

C'mon, let's play! Why are we just standing here?

Lizzie waited and waited, just standing there, hoping Donut would do something "good." Finally, after many minutes, Donut paused. She looked up at Lizzie. And she sat.

Lizzie clicked. “Good girl!” she said. She tossed a treat. Donut jumped up to grab it, gobbled it down in a flash, then immediately sat again. Lizzie clicked. “She gets it!” she said to Aunt Amanda. “I can see it in her eyes.”

“Fantastic,” said Aunt Amanda. “See, your patience paid off. Now, wait for another behavior before you click.”

Lizzie could practically see Donut thinking. The puppy sat. She stared at Lizzie. Lizzie waited for her to offer something new. Donut cocked her head. Then she lay down.

This? Is this what you want?

Lizzie clicked. “Yes!” she said as she tossed a treat. “Such a good girl.”

Later that day, while Aunt Amanda was

cooking dinner, Lizzie sat at the kitchen table with two very tired dogs at her feet. She opened the notebook her aunt had given her.

Training Diary, Day One, she wrote. *Both dogs have responded very well to clicker training. Donut is young but eager to learn. Bowser is an older, very obedient dog. After a few sessions of Step One training, both dogs understood that each click means that a treat is coming soon. Step One is complete. Next, we did Step Two, helping the dogs understand that they need to do something to earn the click. This took a little more work, especially on Donut's part, but they both seem to get it now. Tomorrow we will move on to teaching a simple trick.*

"Donut really did great, didn't she?" Lizzie asked her aunt. "I mean, we can't all be Bowser and be perfect right away, but for a puppy this young?" She reached down and gave Donut a scratch on the head. "Little smartie," she said.

Donut rubbed against Lizzie's hand. Then she lay down with her face between her paws and let out a long sigh.

It's been a lot of fun here, but I sure do miss my people.

Lizzie felt her heart fall at the sight of the sad little face. "Poor Donut," she said. "Don't worry. You're going to see your family tomorrow! And then, well . . ." Lizzie trailed off, knowing all too well how soon Donut would be saying good-bye—probably forever, this time—to her family. Lizzie sighed. "You're such a good girl," she told Donut. "I just wish there was some way we could tell that landlord's wife what a smart, well-behaved, sweet, trainable dog you are. Maybe she would change her mind."

Aunt Amanda stopped chopping onions and stared at Lizzie. "How many brilliant ideas do you have a day, anyway?" she asked.

CHAPTER SEVEN

"What?" Lizzie asked. "What idea?" She loved it when Aunt Amanda praised her, but she honestly didn't know what her brilliant idea was.

"I can't believe I haven't already done it," said Aunt Amanda. She put down her knife and wiped her hands on a dish towel. "I have that landlord's e-mail address! I can send him a note. I've done it before, vouching for clients' dogs. Sometimes it actually works!"

She pulled her laptop out of one of the bags Lizzie had helped carry in that morning and sat down at the table with Lizzie, dinner forgotten. "Some landlords are just worried that a dog will be a barker or mean or destructive. Nobody wants a dog like that on their property. If they get a guarantee from me that the dog has no behavior problems, sometimes landlords are willing to take a chance and let a tenant have a dog."

"But didn't you say that Mac's landlord never even asked you for a reference?" Lizzie asked.

"He didn't," said Aunt Amanda, tapping her fingers as she waited for her laptop to boot up. "But that doesn't mean I can't give him one."

Lizzie felt Donut leaning against her legs, under the table. When she reached down to pet her, she could feel that Donut was trembling.

Things seem serious all of a sudden. What's up?

"It's okay, girl," Lizzie said. She hated to see the puppy so worried. Dogs always knew when something was happening. Lizzie remembered one time when Mom had rushed off because she'd heard that the Bean had fallen and hit his head at day care. Buddy had been anxious, pacing along with Lizzie and Charles and their Dad while they waited to hear if he was okay. (He was. The Bean was, as Charles said, "a tough little dude.")

"Anyway, I can't write directly to the landlord's wife, but I can write to him and give Donut a really great reference. You can help." Aunt Amanda peered at the screen and clicked a few times. "Ah, there it is. His address. Now, let's see what we want to say to him." She bent over her keyboard and began to poke at the keys. Lizzie could see that Aunt Amanda wasn't a fast typist like Mom. She was more of a one-finger-at-a-time typist.

"How about if you say what to write and I type it in?" Lizzie asked, her fingers itching to race along the keys. Mom had taught her how to type fast, too.

Aunt Amanda looked up. "Sure," she said. She pushed the laptop over to Lizzie and got up to pace around the kitchen. "Dear—what's his name again?"

Lizzie checked. "Mr. Mueller. Joseph," she said.

"Dear Mr. Mueller," said Aunt Amanda. "I know that you have already made the decision not to allow Mac and Wanda Cartwright to have their dog, Donut, in your rental unit."

Lizzie typed as fast as she could. "Yup," she said, when she had that much.

"I am writing to ask you to give Donut a chance," Aunt Amanda said. "Mac and Wanda are the nicest people, and their dog is one of the smartest, best-behaved pets I have ever had the pleasure to work with."

Lizzie typed some more. "Good. Um, maybe you need to remind them who you are? Otherwise you're just a name they don't know."

Aunt Amanda nodded. “I own a doggy day-care center called Bowser’s Backyard, and Donut has been coming to me for day care, boarding, and training since she was eight weeks old.” She stopped pacing and bent over to look at Donut under the table. “Isn’t that right?” she asked. “We’ve known each other since you were just an itty-bitty girl.”

Donut thumped her tail and squirmed out from under the table for some pats. Like all dogs, she loved Aunt Amanda. She snuffled at Aunt Amanda’s hand, then lay down again with her head on her paws.

You’re so kind, and you smell so good. And you give out such good treats. But—you’re not my people.

Aunt Amanda finished up the letter with a few more words about how gentle and sweet Donut was, and told the landlord he could contact her with any further questions. "Good," she said, when Lizzie read it back. "Let's let it sit while we eat dinner, in case we think of anything to add. Meanwhile, as long as my laptop is out, maybe you could upload the videos we took today of our training sessions?" She handed Lizzie her phone. Then after one more hug for Donut, she washed her hands and went back to chopping onions.

Lizzie wasn't sure exactly how to upload the videos, but since Aunt Amanda had so much confidence in her, she gave it a try. It turned out to be easy.

"Look at Donut," she said as she watched the video of their Step Two training. Aunt Amanda came over to look over her shoulder.

"She's like a little sponge, just soaking everything up," said Aunt Amanda, shaking her head.

"You could teach this puppy how to do just about anything."

Lizzie wished it was that easy to teach people to give dogs a chance. Then Donut could stay with her people, where she belonged.

CHAPTER EIGHT

After dinner, Aunt Amanda and Lizzie collapsed on the couch. Bowser climbed up next to Aunt Amanda, and Donut curled up between Lizzie and her aunt. At Camp Bowser (and at Aunt Amanda's house), dogs were welcome on the couch. "I'm not up for any more training tonight," said Aunt Amanda as she petted both dogs. "Let's just watch a movie. You can pick one for all of us."

"Buddy's favorite movie is *The Adventures of Milo and Otis*," said Lizzie.

"Perfect," said Aunt Amanda. "I even own that one on DVD. Should be right there, under the TV."

Lizzie went to look for it. On her way back, she checked Aunt Amanda's laptop for the tenth time. They had sent the e-mail right after dinner. Why wasn't that landlord writing back to say that he'd changed his mind?

Lizzie checked again later, when she woke to see that all four of them had fallen asleep half-way through the movie. Still no e-mail. She even checked in the middle of the night, when Donut woke her up, needing to go out for a pee.

There was no e-mail waiting for them when they got up in the morning, either. She checked again after they walked the dogs. Nothing. Lizzie tried to hide her frustration, but she could tell that Donut was starting to notice how stressed she was feeling. The puppy crawled under the table again while they were having breakfast. Every so often, she would snuffle at Lizzie's hand and look up at her with serious eyes. She put a gentle paw on Lizzie's knee.

Aren't you the one who's always telling me not to worry?

"Aw, she wants you to feel better," said Aunt Amanda, noticing.

"I know," said Lizzie. "She's really tuned in to people's feelings. I keep thinking how great Donut must be with Mac and Wanda's kids." It was so frustrating that she couldn't just make that landlord do what she wanted him to do: Say yes to Donut!

"Can you stay up here with Donut for a bit?" Aunt Amanda asked as they cleaned up after breakfast. "Before we get started today, I want to take Bowser down to the lake for twenty minutes, to work on the canoe training."

"Of course," said Lizzie, bending down to scoop

Donut into her arms. She was just small enough that you could still pick her up, even though she was heavy.

"Maybe you can set up the tripod and get things ready for our morning lesson," said her aunt. "I'll be back soon, and we should be able to get in some good training time before we have to pack up and go home." She handed Lizzie her phone. "And stay off that computer!" She smiled and gave Lizzie a hug. "Try not to worry."

Lizzie checked her aunt's e-mail one more time. Nothing, of course. Then she took Donut onto the Pooch Porch. "Let's get things set up out here," she said. Donut pranced along, looking up at Lizzie.

How can I help? What can I do?

It only took a minute to get the phone set up on the tripod, since they'd already figured that part out the day before. Lizzie looked at Donut. "Want to play a game?" she asked. She felt like she and Donut were both pretty good at this clicker training. Maybe she could surprise her aunt with a new trick.

They'd already cut up a bunch of roast beef for treats, and Lizzie took some out of the cooler. What should she teach Donut? Maybe shake hands? That was the next trick after sit, which the puppy already knew. Lizzie got ready with the clicker and stood patiently, waiting to see what Donut would do. Donut looked at her, tilting her head. Then she seemed to remember yesterday's lesson.

Oh, right! I know what works.

She sat, bumping her little butt down solidly. Lizzie clicked. "Good girl," she said, giving Donut a treat. Then she waited again. Since Donut was already sitting, the puppy had to figure out what to do next. She stared at Lizzie and tilted her head this way and that. Then she pawed at the air.

"Yes!" Lizzie said, before she remembered to click. Then she clicked, and gave Donut a treat. She reminded herself to be careful. You had to be just right on the timing with the clicker.

Donut pawed at the air again. Lizzie thought it looked just like she was trying to give a high five. "Yes!" she said again, clicking at the same time. "High five!" Why not? That was even better than shake. She gave Donut a treat. Right away, Donut pawed at the air one more time, but this time she did it with both paws, jumping up on Lizzie.

Whee, this is fun!

Surprised, Lizzie clicked. "Oops," she said. "I mean, no!" She never should have clicked for such naughty behavior. "Donut, no jumping." She took a step back. "What was *that*?" she asked Donut, who was sitting again, looking up at her with a bewildered expression.

Did I do something wrong? I thought that clicking sound meant I did something right!

"Let's try again," Lizzie said. "High five, Donut!" She held up a hand as a signal. Donut pawed at the air, but then just as Lizzie clicked, the puppy jumped right up and onto Lizzie, both paws on Lizzie's knees. This time, she almost knocked Lizzie over.

"Oh, no," Lizzie groaned, when she'd found her balance. Somehow, she had managed to teach Donut to do something that good dogs did not do. This clicker training was harder than it looked. Lizzie shook her head, putting Donut back into a sit. “This is terrible,” she said. “This is not the kind of behavior that makes landlords happy.”

“What’s that?” Aunt Amanda asked, opening the screen door. She and Bowser came onto the porch.

“Uh . . . nothing,” said Lizzie. “I was just saying how happy that landlord would be if he could see what a good girl Donut is.” Maybe the puppy wouldn’t jump up again. Maybe Lizzie would never have to tell Aunt Amanda what a mess she’d made of things.

Aunt Amanda smiled. “And Bowser is a good boy,” she said. “Guess what? I actually got him to sit in the canoe for ten seconds. I think with another good session he’ll be ready to ride around the pond with me.” She took Bowser off for a nap in the yoga room, then came back, ready to dive into a lesson with Donut.

“Ready?” Aunt Amanda asked. She started the video, then came to stand near Lizzie and Donut.

Lizzie crossed her fingers, hoping Donut would forget her new "trick." But the phone camera had only been running for a few seconds before Donut, who was still very excited, jumped up on Lizzie.

Aunt Amanda gasped. "What happened?" she asked. "I've never seen Donut do anything like that before."

CHAPTER NINE

Lizzie hung her head. She sniffed, holding back the tears she felt building up. “I did it,” she confessed. This time she wanted to get the truth out right away. “It’s totally my fault.”

Aunt Amanda touched Lizzie’s shoulder. “Come on, now,” she said. “It can’t be that bad. What happened?”

“I taught her to jump up!” Lizzie said. “I mean, not on purpose. I just clicked at the wrong time. Twice. And she’s such a fast learner. And now I made her into a bad dog that no landlord will ever want.” She couldn’t hold back the tears anymore. She started to sob.

Aunt Amanda pulled Lizzie into her arms. Donut wriggled her way into the hug, snuffling and licking at Lizzie's face.

Don't cry! Please don't cry! I can't take it when people cry!

"Honey, don't cry," said Aunt Amanda, rocking Lizzie in her arms. "It's not the end of the world. We can fix it. Remember what you just said: Donut learns fast. She can unlearn fast, too." She gave Donut a kiss on the nose. "Isn't that right, smart girl?"

"But how?" Lizzie asked.

"With the clicker, of course," said Aunt Amanda. "I think I know how. Let's film this. It could be really useful—if it works!" She laughed. "Actually, it'll be useful even if it doesn't work. I've probably learned more from my mistakes than from anything I did right. C'mon, Donut," she said, smacking her leg. Donut trotted after her.

Lizzie followed them.

"You run the camera," said Aunt Amanda. "I'll be the trainer this time. The thing about clicker training is that, while the first steps are easy, it gets harder. It can take a lot of experience—and a lot of mistakes—to get the timing just right." She grabbed some treats. Donut was still at her heels, following her closely. Aunt Amanda stopped and stood completely still. She didn't say a word. Lizzie could see that her aunt was waiting to see what Donut did.

Thankfully, the puppy did not jump up. Instead, she sat. Aunt Amanda clicked and gave her a treat. "Good sit," she said. Then she waited some more. She was very calm, very quiet, not even really looking at Donut.

Donut cocked her head and stared at Aunt Amanda.

Aunt Amanda basically ignored her.

For a second, Lizzie wondered if Donut would jump up to get her attention. Instead, Donut sighed and lay down, putting her chin on her paws.

Well, this is kinda boring. Guess I'll take a break.

Instantly, Aunt Amanda clicked. "Good girl," she said, giving Donut a treat. She looked at Lizzie and the camera. "That's exactly what I wanted her to do. I wanted her to get the idea that the best way to get my attention is to lie down, not jump up." Aunt Amanda took a few steps and called Donut over. Then she ran through the whole sequence again. "See, if I stay very still and calm, she's unlikely to jump. Instead, she'll get bored and lie down, and then I can reward her for that." Donut did exactly what Aunt Amanda had predicted, and again, the instant she lay down, there was a click and a treat.

"That's amazing," said Lizzie. Aunt Amanda really was a professional.

"Like I said, I've made a lot of mistakes along the way," said Aunt Amanda. "And you will, too. You're already a very good dog trainer, but I have a feeling you'll be a great one someday."

Lizzie felt tears come to her eyes again. That was silly. Why did she feel like crying? Aunt Amanda was saying something nice, after all. It was all just a little overwhelming: Donut's sad story of being separated from her people; the hard work of training; the awful (but maybe not permanent) mistake she had made—and now this. "Really?" she said.

Then she heard it.

The *bing* that meant a new e-mail had arrived on Aunt Amanda's laptop.

Aunt Amanda heard it, too. They both ran for the kitchen, Donut at their heels.

Aunt Amanda got there first and opened the e-mail. "It's from him, from the landlord," she said. Lizzie looked over her shoulder, and they read together, out loud. "Thanks for your letter regarding Donut. She sounds like a very excellent dog," it said. "Unfortunately, I still can't convince my wife to allow her on the property."

Aunt Amanda leaned back and threw up her hands. "Ugh. Well, I guess that sounds pretty final."

"No!" said Lizzie. "Come on. Don't give up yet. We have to persuade them somehow." She knelt

down to give Donut a big hug. "I mean, this dog is one in a million. She has a wonderful family, who loves her like crazy. She's sweet and beautiful and so, so smart." She squeezed Donut, maybe a little too hard. Donut squirmed in her arms, and Lizzie let her go. She watched her amble over to the water bowl and take a slurping drink. Donut was so cute. "Wait," said Lizzie. "What if we sent them one of the training videos we made? Honestly, how could anybody resist once they see how cute and smart she is?"

Aunt Amanda, who had been slumped over her keyboard, turned around and grinned at her. "The Idea Queen strikes again," she said. "Why not? At this point, we have nothing to lose, do we?" She got up and offered Lizzie her seat. "You type." Then she began to dictate:

"Thank you for your note. I understand. Some people are not used to dogs, or not good dogs anyway. Please do me one favor and show the attached video to your wife."

Lizzie attached the video from yesterday's Step Two training. Then she looked at Aunt Amanda, eyebrows raised. "Send?" she asked.

"Send," said Aunt Amanda.

CHAPTER TEN

"Well, I guess that's that," said Lizzie as she closed the lid of Aunt Amanda's laptop later that day. She had just checked Aunt Amanda's e-mail one last time before they climbed into the already-packed SUV to head home. The weekend at Camp Bowser was over, and there was still no solution to the Donut problem. The landlord had not responded to the e-mail with the video attached. "I can't think of anything else to try," she said, "unless we drive Donut all the way out to California so his wife can meet her in person and see how wonderful she is."

Aunt Amanda laughed. "That sounds like a fun road trip," she said. She patted Lizzie on the shoulder. "Listen, we did our best. And look at everything we accomplished this weekend. I've got my clicker training workshop just about ready to go, thanks to your amazing help. And Bowser took his first ride in the canoe!"

Lizzie couldn't help laughing, too, remembering how noble Bowser had looked riding in the front of Aunt Amanda's red canoe, earlier that day. He was like one of those carved figureheads on old ships, his head held high and his ears flapping in the breeze. Lizzie had caught it all on video, filming from the shore. "I think Bowser actually enjoys the canoe now," she said as she climbed into the SUV and buckled up for the ride home.

Both dogs were tucked into their crates in the way-back, and Lizzie was sure they would snooze all the way home. She might even take a little nap, herself. It had been a busy morning. Besides the canoe ride, each dog had gone through two more sessions of clicker training.

Bowser had learned to squirm his way under a low table, something Lizzie could not imagine Buddy ever doing. Buddy was afraid to even fetch one of his toys if it went partway under a chair. "Most dogs are like that," Aunt Amanda had said. "But with clicker training, it's easy to teach them that there's nothing to be afraid of—just like Bowser learned to get into the canoe."

She had also taught Bowser to spin around in a circle, which he seemed to think was lots of fun. He galumphed around and around, grinning a big doggy grin. Lizzie had a feeling that video would be very popular.

Donut had learned what Aunt Amanda had called an "emergency down." That meant the pup would drop to the ground (or floor) the second she heard the word "down," no matter how far away she was from the person speaking the command. She'd even done it with Lizzie out of sight, calling out "down!" from behind the porch door.

"It's one of the most useful commands to have," said Aunt Amanda. "I wish every dog owner would teach their dog how to drop on command. It can really come in handy."

She had also taught Donut how to sit up pretty with her paws held up. It was the cutest thing. Lizzie wanted to send another video to the landlord, but Aunt Amanda talked her out of it. "Let's wait and see if he responds to the other one first," she said.

Lizzie was already planning to teach Buddy some new tricks. She could hardly wait to get home and start clicker training with him. And if Donut was going to stay with the Petersons, at least for a while, Lizzie could keep working with her, too. Donut had not jumped up one single time since Aunt Amanda had undone Lizzie's mistake, and Lizzie was sure there was plenty she could teach the smart little pup.

Aunt Amanda pulled the SUV into the parking lot at Bowser's Backyard. "Oh, check it out, Donut! Mac and Wanda are already here to pick you up," she said, looking into the rearview mirror at the pup in her crate. "The kids are here, too." But Lizzie could see that Donut already knew that. She had sprung up in her crate as soon as they slowed down, and she was staring out the window with her ears perked up. She whined and pawed at the crate.

My people! I hear them! I smell them! Let me out. I can't wait to be with them again.

As soon as Aunt Amanda stopped the SUV, Lizzie unbuckled and went to let Donut out, snapping her leash on before she released her from the crate. Donut leapt out of the SUV and dragged Lizzie at full speed toward Mac and Wanda and their two children.

"Donut!" cried the little boy. He knelt down and opened his arms, and she ran right into his hug.

"Oh, Donut," said his sister, "we missed you so much."

Lizzie looked at Mac and Wanda, who stood watching with their arms around each other. Once again, Mac was crying. Lizzie knew it must be very painful for him. How awful that these kids were going to have to give up their dog.

"I'm really sorry," she said to him. "We tried to convince your landlord, but it didn't work."

He smiled at her, through his tears. "Actually, it did!" he said. "We just got an e-mail from Mr. Mueller, about a half an hour ago. He told us all about the video you sent, and how he showed it to his wife. I guess he finally wore her down, and she agreed to let Donut come with us—'on a trial basis.'" He made quote marks with his fingers.

Aunt Amanda grinned and gave Lizzie a high five. "Yes!" she said. "We know how that will go. Anybody who gets to know this dog falls in love right away."

Donut wriggled and squirmed as she licked the kids' faces. She wagged her tail and let out little woofs—but Lizzie was glad to see that she did not jump up, not once, even though the moment was so exciting. Lizzie was sad to know that she was going to have to say good-bye to Donut—but could there be a happier ending for this puppy's story? She was going to be able to stay with her perfect family, after all. "Congratulations," she said to Mac and Wanda. "I'm so happy for all of you."

PUPPY TIPS

Clicker training has been around for a long time. Believe it or not, it started as a way to train dolphins! Now there are many people who use it to train dogs, and it really can work like magic. An adult can help you find some videos like the ones Lizzie watched. You'll be amazed to see how quickly dogs can learn! If you try it yourself, keep in mind that it can be very challenging to get the timing just right, as Lizzie found out. It's probably best to find a dog trainer or a class nearby so you and your dog can learn from an expert.

Click!

Dear Reader,

I tried clicker training with my dog, Zipper, when he was just a puppy. He was terrified by the sound, and at the time, I had never heard of the tricks (muffling the clicker, hiding it behind your back) that Lizzie learned. I gave up clicker training until I was working on this book, and then I tried it again. Now, at eight years old, Zipper is a little less of a 'fraidy-dog (although certain things, like a big fly buzzing around his head, can still scare him). This time, it worked much better. I used the clicker to teach him to stay on the trail when we are out hiking and he is off the leash, and it worked really well. I'm going to keep experimenting with the clicker. Zipper may be an older dog, but he can still learn new tricks!

Yours from the Puppy Place,

Ellen Miles

THE PUPPY PLACE

DON'T MISS THE FIRST PUPPY PLACE ADVENTURE!

Here's a peek at Goldie

Charles woke up with a bad feeling in his stomach. Why? For a minute, he couldn't figure it out. Then he rolled over and looked at his clock. It was 3:46 A.M., and Charles could hear the loud *deedle-deedle-dee* of his dad's pager going off. Mr. Peterson was a volunteer fireman. When his pager went off, there was a fire somewhere in town.

Charles listened to his dad's footsteps going

downstairs. Then he heard the slam of a truck door and an engine starting up. He lay there for a while, worrying a little. He decided to stay awake until his dad came home.

But he must have fallen asleep, because when he woke up again, the sun was shining and his clock said it was 7:16. Charles rubbed his eyes and climbed out of bed. Then he raced down to the kitchen and looked out the window.

Dad's red pickup was not in the driveway.

Mom was making French toast while the Bean—Charles's little brother—crawled around on the floor by her feet. The smell of cinnamon made Charles's mouth water. "Is Dad—" Charles began.

"Dad's fine," Mom said. "He called a little while ago. There was a big fire, but everyone is okay."

Charles let out a big breath. It was cool to have a fireman dad, but scary sometimes, too.

"He'll be home soon," Mom told Charles.

"Where was the fire?" asked Lizzie, scuffing her slippers as she shuffled into the kitchen. She rubbed her eyes and yawned. Lizzie was Charles's older sister. It always took her a long time to wake up.

"Out at a farm in Middletown," Mom said.

At this, Lizzie's eyes popped open. "Were any animals hurt?" she asked.

Mom shook her head. "I don't think so." She flipped a slice of French toast. "Set the table, okay?" Mom asked.

That *proved* that everything was okay. What could be more normal than doing chores?

Since there was no reason to worry, Charles decided to ask his favorite question, the one he asked every single morning.

"So *why* can't we have a dog?" he asked.

ABOUT THE AUTHOR

Ellen Miles loves dogs, which is why she has a great time writing the Puppy Place books. And guess what? She loves cats, too! (In fact, her very first pet was a beautiful tortoiseshell cat named Jenny.) That's why she came up with the Kitty Corner series. Ellen lives in Vermont and loves to be outdoors with her dog, Zipper, every day, walking, biking, skiing, or swimming, depending on the season. She also loves to read, cook, explore her beautiful state, play with dogs, and hang out with friends and family.

Visit Ellen at ellenmiles.net.